N
c   e have you been?

305/2

Nicolas, where have you been?

by Leo Lionni

Alfred A. Knopf ❧ New York

At the edge of the Great Meadow four little field mice were nibbling berries.

"Look for the red ones," said Elodie.

"They're the sweetest and juiciest," said Henry.

"Because they're ripe," said William.

But all they could find were pale pink berries that were neither sweet nor juicy. The ripe red ones had already been picked.

"The birds got here before you," said Uncle Raymond, who was watching them.

"That's not fair," said Nicolas. "Why should they get the best berries? Down with the birds!"

"Down with the birds!" all the little mice shouted.

Then and there Nicolas decided to look for a berry patch that the birds had not yet discovered. He would find the sweetest and juiciest berries in the whole world. Without telling anyone, he set out across the Great Meadow. He walked on and on, seeing nothing but the tall grass that surrounded him.

At last Nicolas reached a clearing. He scanned the horizon
but there wasn't a berry in sight. Then suddenly he heard
the noise of flapping wings. He looked up. A big, ugly bird
swooped down on him.

Before Nicolas could run back into the tall grass and hide,
the bird grabbed him with its sharp claws and carried him
up into the sky.

"Help! Help!" Nicolas shrieked. He twisted and wiggled wildly, and the bird lost its grip. Nicolas plunged through the air.

He landed in a nest where three little birds were dozing. They jumped up. "Who are you?" they asked.

"I am Nicolas, a field mouse." And he told them about his adventure.

"Stay with us," said the birds. "You can tell us mouse stories and we will tell you all about birds."

Then their mother appeared with a worm.

"Mother," said one of the little birds, "this is Nicolas, a field mouse. May he stay with us?"

"Of course," said the mother bird. "But what do little field mice eat?"

"Berries," said Nicolas. "Field mice like nuts and corn and berries. Ripe red berries."

The mother bird flew off and soon returned with a bright red berry. Nicolas couldn't believe his eyes. And it was the sweetest berry he had ever tasted.

The days flew by. Nicolas ate berries to his heart's content. He and the little birds peeped and tweeted mouse songs, bird songs, and funny stories, and at night they cuddled up against the mother bird's soft down.

But one morning Nicolas woke up to discover that his friends had flown away. They had left a big pile of berries in the nest, but Nicolas was too sad to eat.

Nicolas knew that the time had come for him
to leave the high nest. Fearfully he climbed
down the tree, from branch to branch, from
twig to twig.

When he finally reached the ground, he found himself
face to face with Elodie, Henry, and William.

"Nicolas!" they shouted excitedly. "Where have you
been? We have been looking all over for you!"

Nicolas began to tell what had happened. But when
he told how the big, ugly bird swooped down and
grabbed him with its claws, the others became furious.

And before Nicolas could add another word they shouted,
"Down with the birds! War on the birds! War on all the birds!"
They shouted on and on.

"Let me finish!" Nicolas insisted desperately. "Let me finish my story!"

When the mice had finally quieted down, Nicolas told them about the nest, the birds, the songs, and the stories. Little by little the anger faded from their faces.

Suddenly they shouted, "Nicolas! Look behind you!"

Nicolas turned around. There were the birds. In their beaks they carried the ripe red berries he knew so well. "For you," they said.

Just then Uncle Raymond appeared from behind a tree. He smiled and slowly raised his cane. "That shows you," he said. "One bad bird doesn't make a flock." Then he joined the others.

It was a feast. Everyone, including Uncle Raymond, agreed that the berries were the most delicious they had ever tasted.

Leo Lionni is internationally acclaimed as an artist, designer, sculptor, art director, and creator of animal fables for children. He is the recipient of the 1984 American Institute of Graphic Arts Gold Medal and is a four-time Caldecott Honor Book winner for *Inch by Inch, Swimmy, Alexander and the Wind-Up Mouse,* and *Frederick*. His picture books are noted for being both playful and serious and are distinguished by their graphic simplicity and brilliant use of collage.

Lionni was born in Amsterdam, Holland. He studied there, in Belgium, the U.S.A., Switzerland, and Italy, and received a Ph.D. in economics from the University of Genoa. In 1939 he came to this country with his wife, Nora, and their two sons. The Lionnis now divide their time between an apartment in the heart of New York City and a seventeenth-century farmhouse in the Tuscan hills of Italy.

THIS IS A BORZOI BOOK PUBLISHED BY ALFRED A. KNOPF, INC.

Copyright © 1987 by Leo Lionni. All rights reserved under International and Pan-American Copyright Conventions. Published in the United States by Alfred A. Knopf, Inc., New York, and simultaneously in Canada by Random House of Canada Limited, Toronto. Distributed by Random House, Inc., New York. Manufactured in the United States of America   10 9 8 7 6 5 4 3 2 1

Library of Congress Cataloging-in-Publication Data: Lionni, Leo. Nicolas, where have you been? Summary: Mishap turns to adventure as a young mouse learns that all birds aren't the enemies he thought they were. [1. Birds—Fiction. 2. Mice—Fiction] I. Title. PZ7.L6634Ni 1987 [E] 86-18574 ISBN 0-394-88370-5   ISBN 0-394-98370-X (lib. bdg.)